Coz and Lolo like to color.
Let's go on a coloring trip
with them!

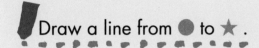 Draw a line from ● to ★.

Example

Eli

Lolo

Coz

Rudi

Let's go to town!

Let's go over the bridges and into town.

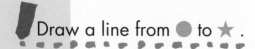 Draw a line from ● to ★.

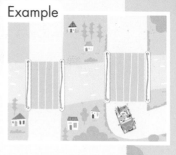
Example

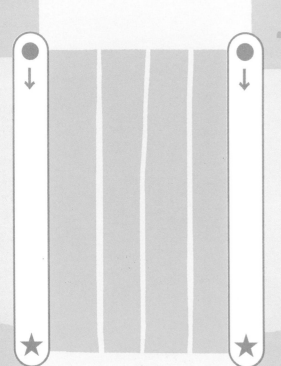

Example

Coz and Lolo meet the mayor.

"Hello, would you please make me a big bow tie

to wear today?" asks the mayor.

Let's draw him a bow tie!

Draw a line from ● to ★.

Example

Lolo needs some ribbons for her hair!

Example

Coz and Lolo meet a pretty lady.
"Hello, would you make my bags
look nice?" asks the pretty lady.

Draw a line from ● to ★ .

Example

Next, they meet the conductor.

"Hello, would you please make some rails for the train?" asks the conductor.

Draw a line from ● to ★.

Example

8

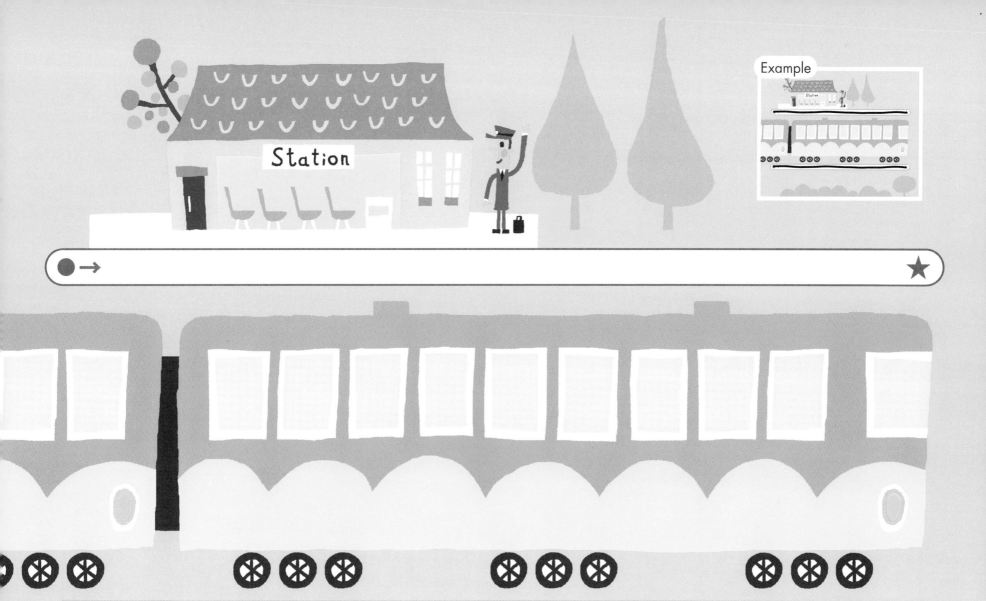

Example

Station

Here is the house of the pretty lady!

She lives by the train station.

Let's make her house look nice!

Draw a line from ● to ★ .

Example

The pretty lady gives them some snacks.

Draw a line from ● to ★.

11

"Please eat the yummy ice cream!" says the pretty lady.

Draw a line from ● to ★.

Example

13

Next, Coz and Lolo go to the grocery store. "Please help us with our tomatoes and eggplants!" says the clerk.

 Draw a line from ● to ★ .

Example

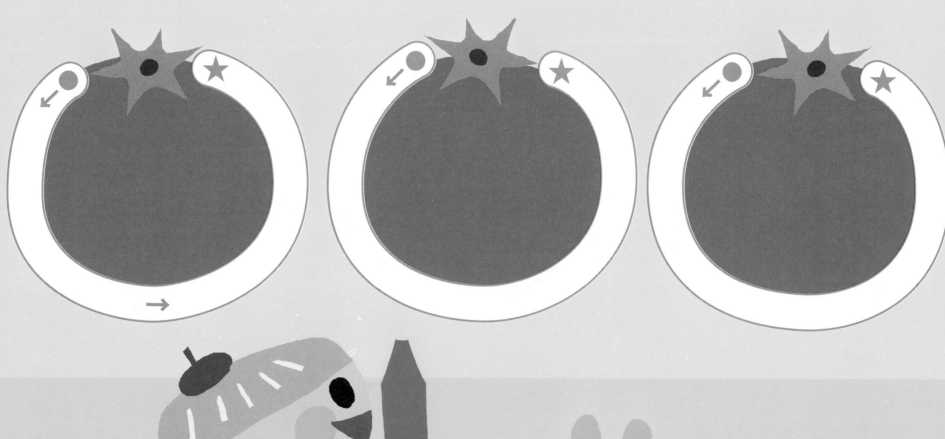

14

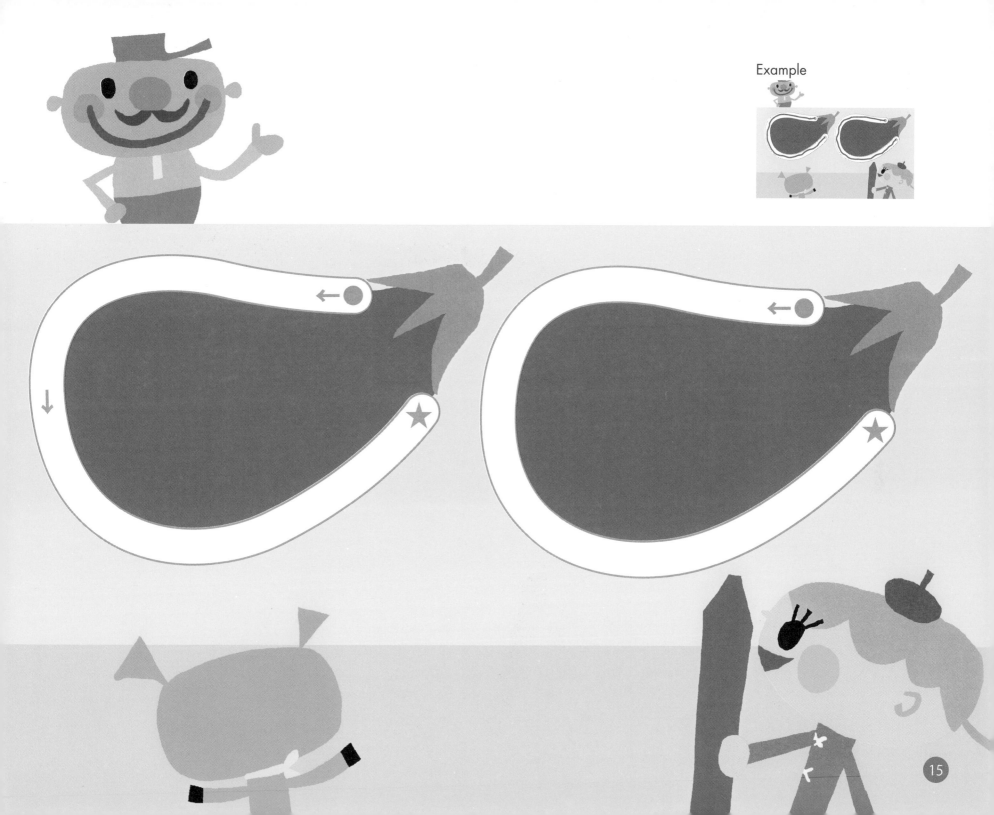

Example

15

"Look at the big rainbow in the sky!" says Coz.

Draw a line from ● to ★.

Example

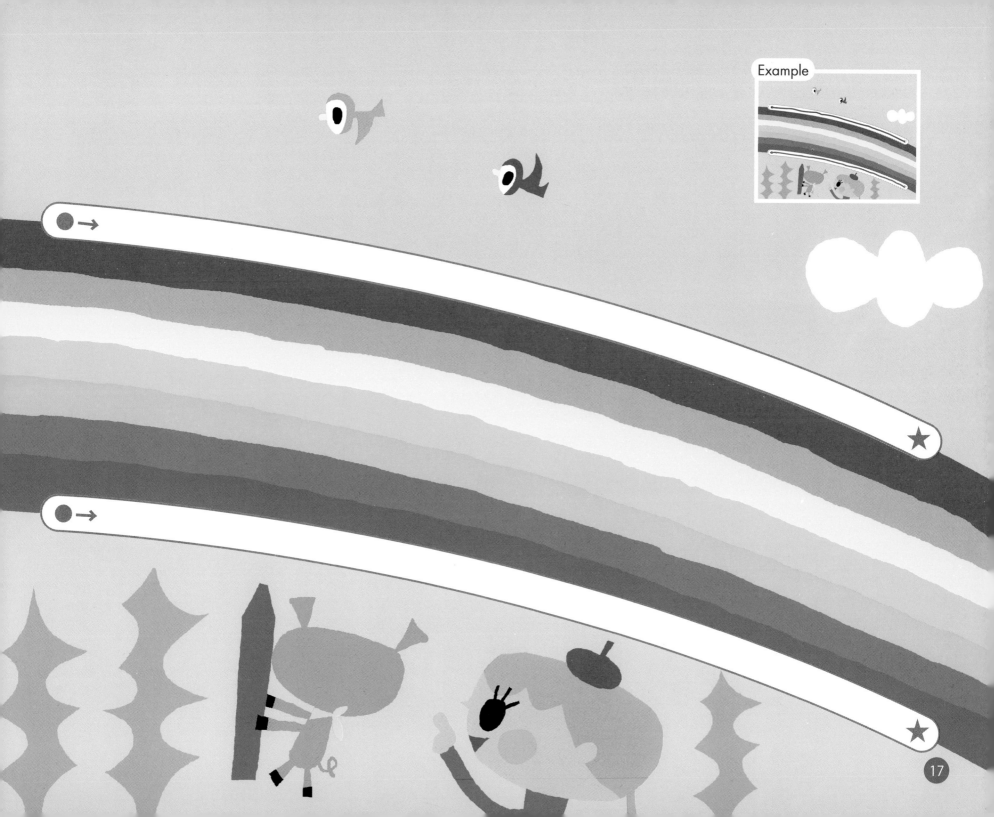

Example

17

Let's go to the mountains!

"What a nice day! Let's go to the mountains," says Coz.

Draw a line from ● to ★ .

18

They find two big waterfalls.

"Look how much water there is!"

says Lolo.

Draw a line from ● to ★.

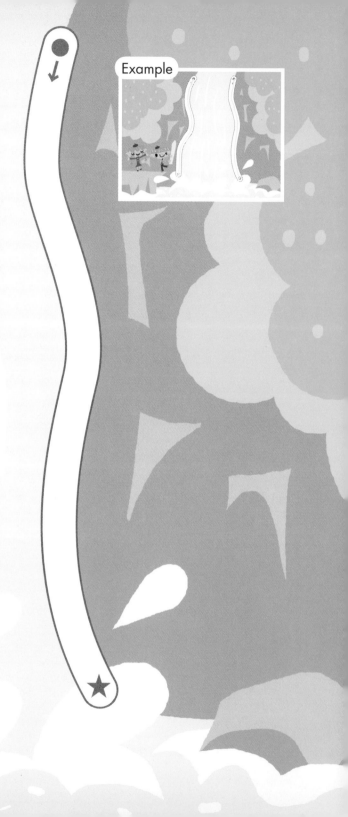

Example

Example

21

Coz and Lolo walk down the path with their friends.

Draw a line from ● to ★ .

Example

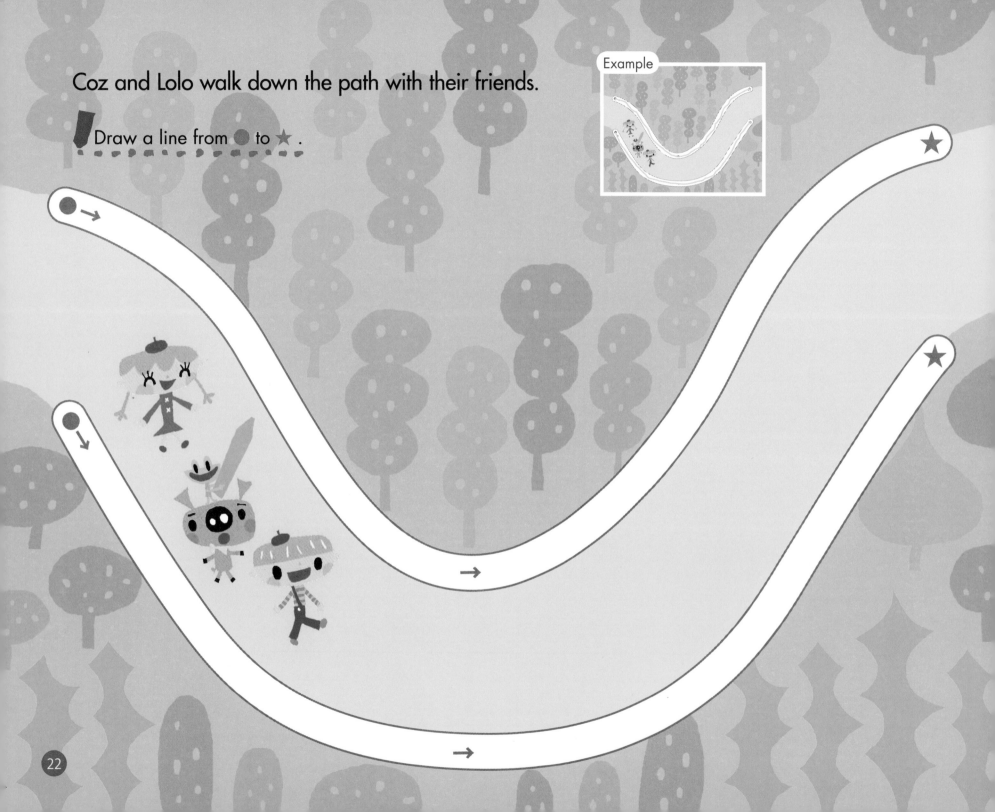

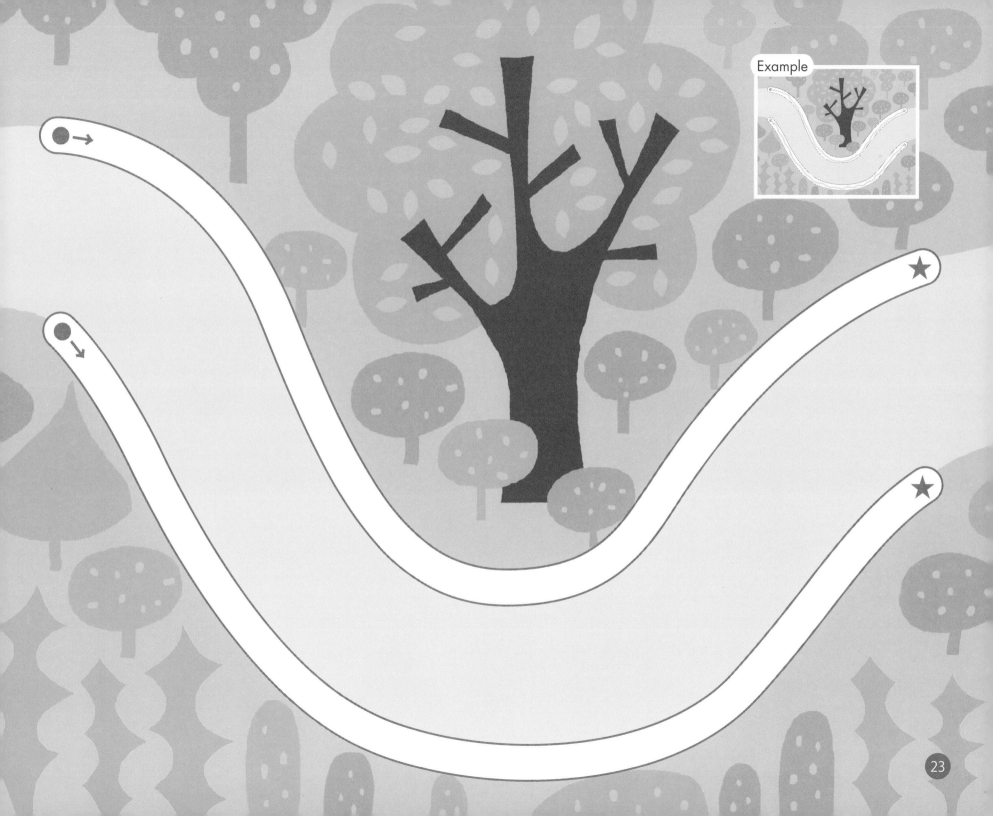

Example

23

They find a big field and rest in the grass.

Draw a line from ● to ★.

24

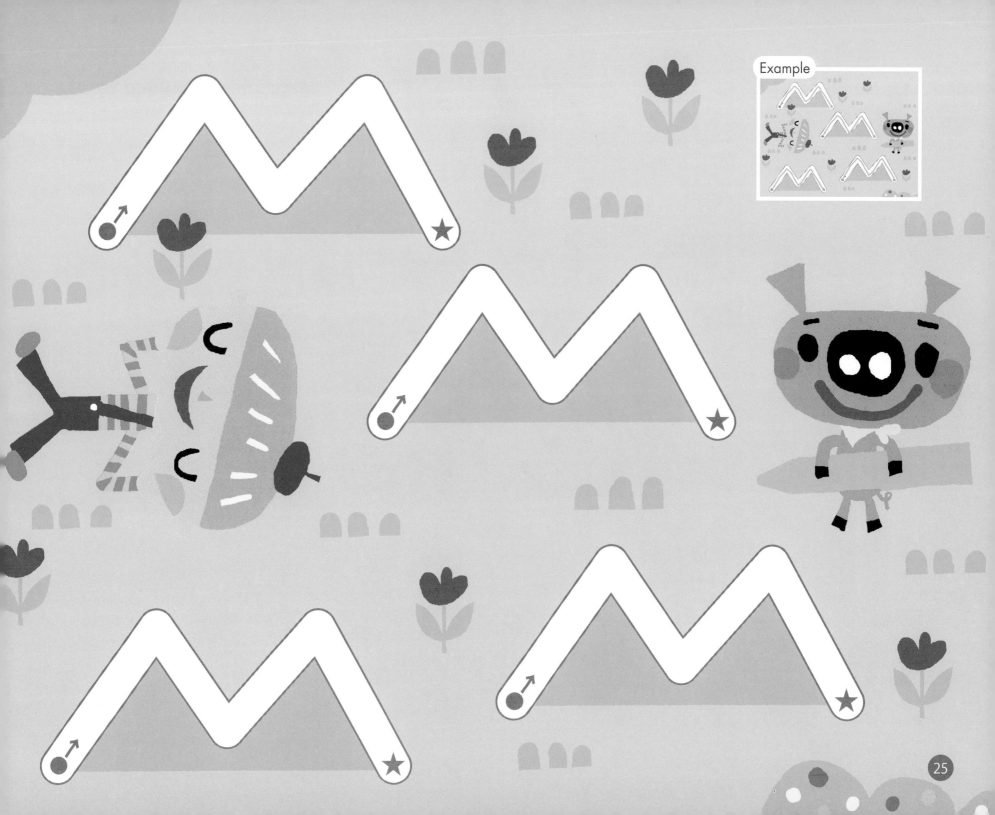

"Oh no, it's raining!" says Lolo.

The thunder rumbles and lightning crashes.

Draw a line from ● to ★.

26

Example

27

"Let's go find a warmer place!" says Coz.

Draw a line from ● to ★.

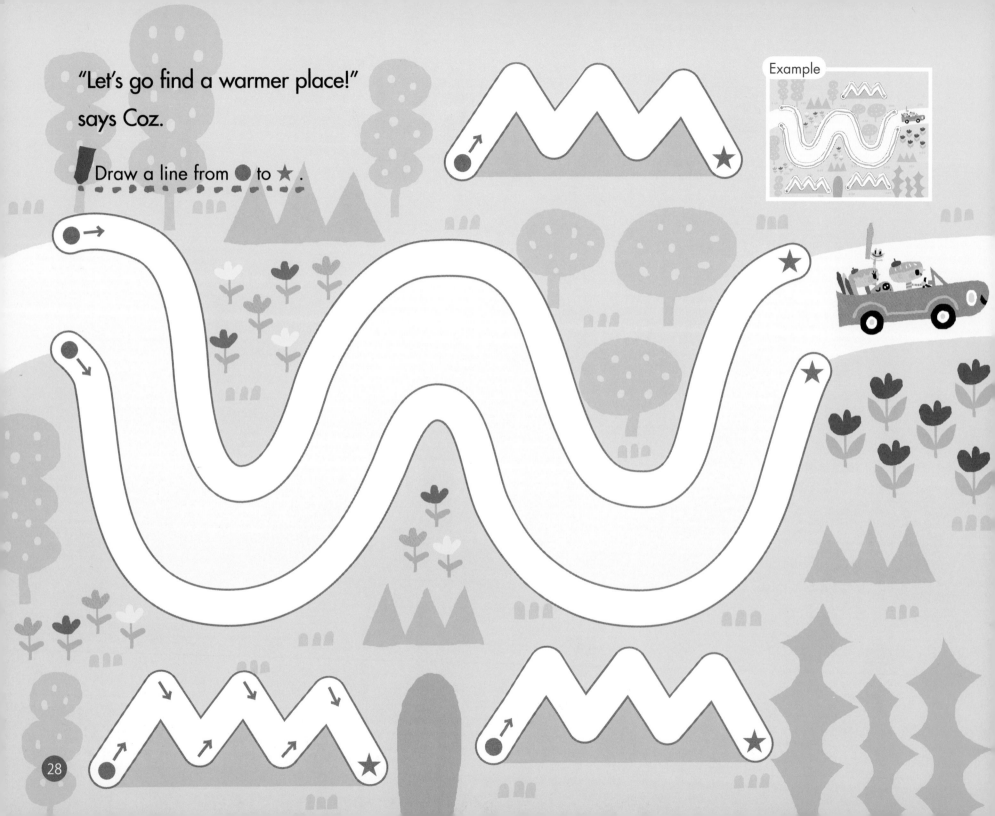

Example

28

Let's go to the forest!

Coz and Lolo go to the forest.

"Look how many trees there are!" says Rudi.

Color the circles with a green crayon.

Example

They walk in the forest.

Coz finds an apple tree! Lolo finds a tangerine tree.

Color the circles with a red or orange crayon.

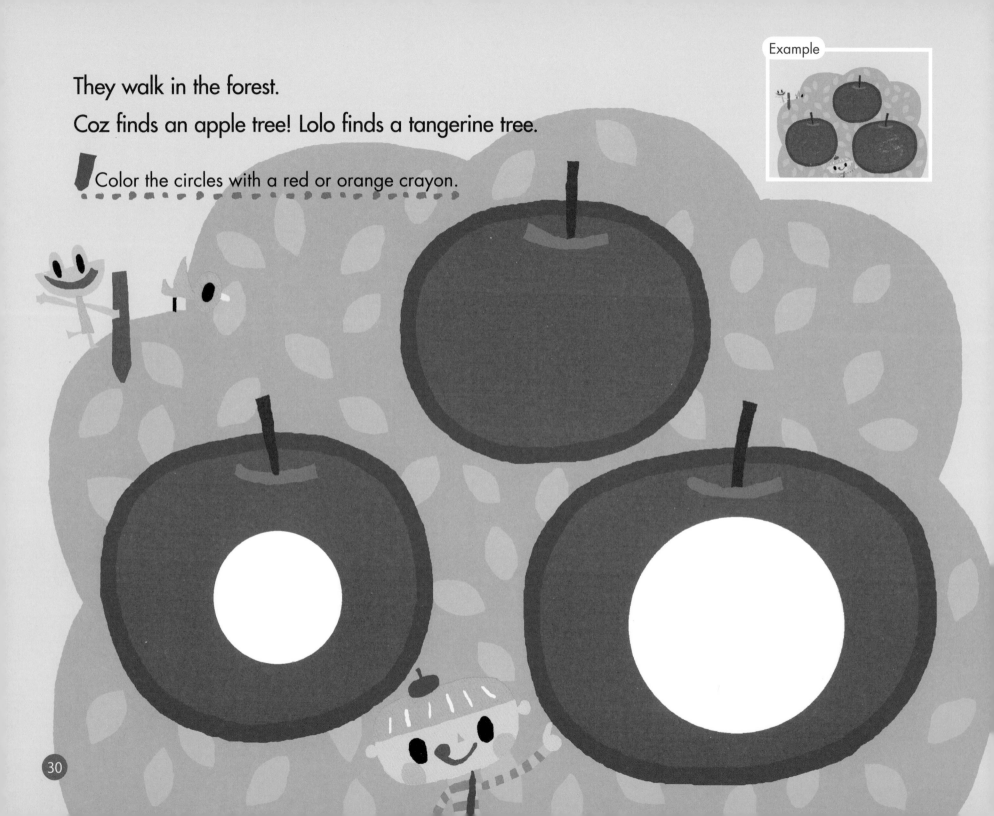

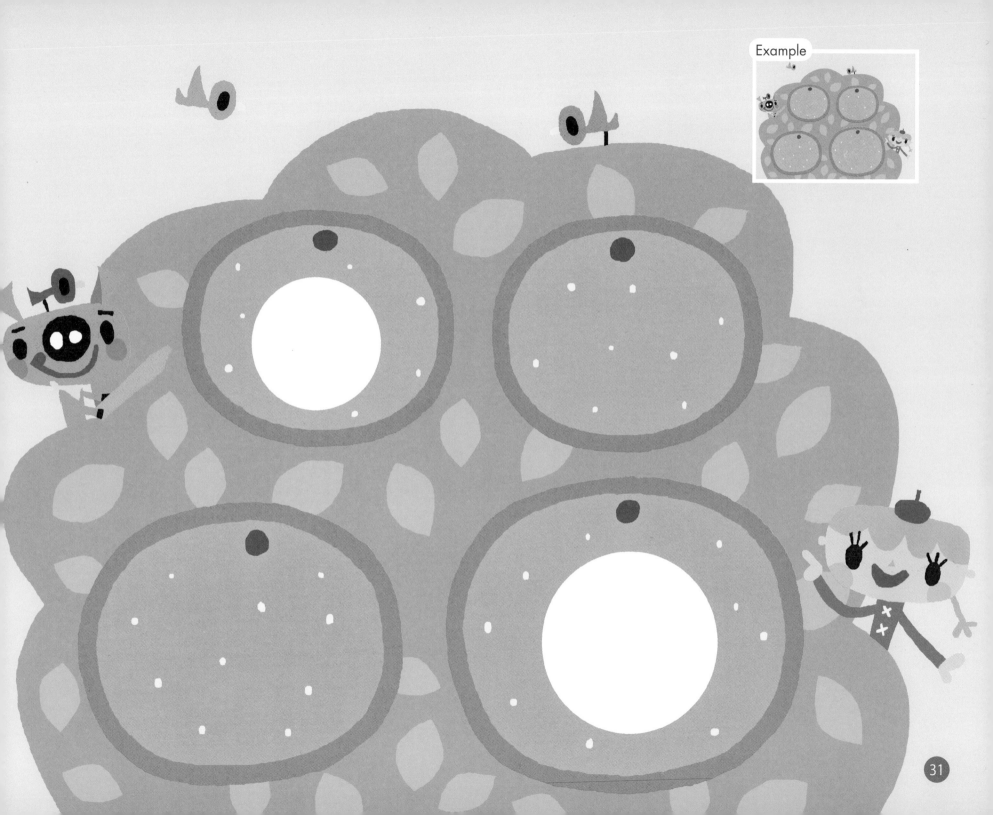

There are red, blue and yellow birds everywhere. "Look at all the pretty birds!" says Lolo.

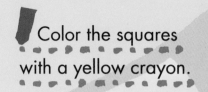 Color the squares with a yellow crayon.

Example

Then Coz and Lolo come out from behind some trees.
They find some pink flamingos and pelicans!

Color the squares with a pink crayon.

Example

Example

35

Lolo sees some monkeys and sloths in the trees.
"Look, Rudi! There are monkeys up there!"
she says.

Color the triangles with a brown crayon.

Example

36

Out in a field, Coz finds
some giraffes and panthers.
Rudi makes a friend!

Finish the patterns
with a brown crayon.

Example

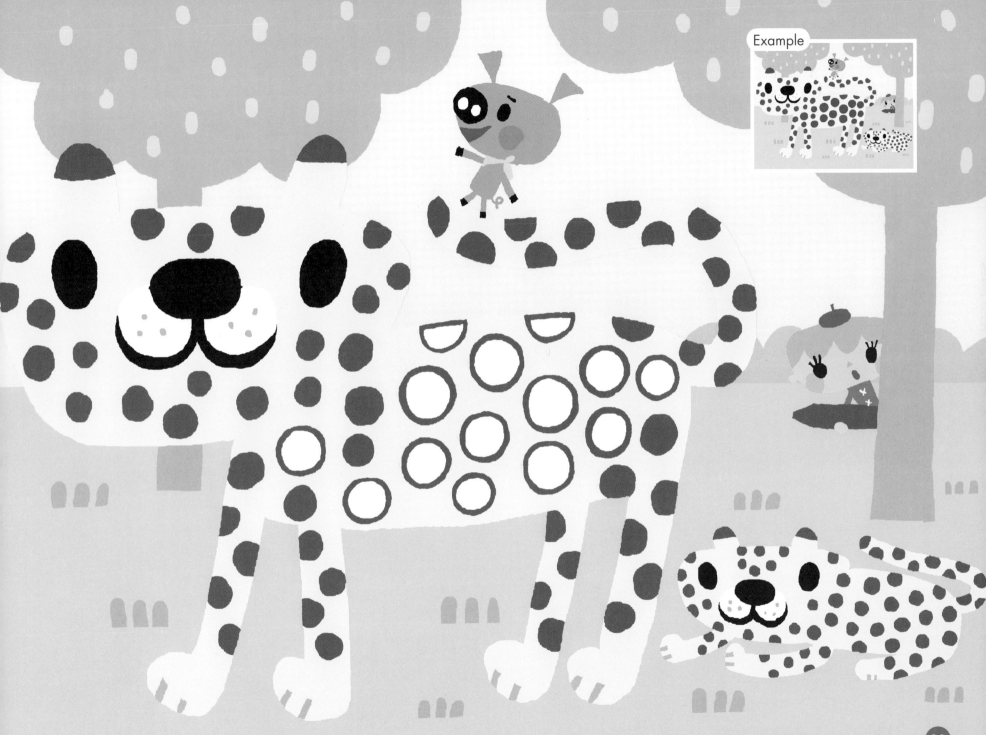

Example

39

Wow, look at the zebras and tigers!

"Watch out Eli!" says Coz.

Finish the patterns with a black or brown crayon.

Example

40

Example

The squirrels and raccoons look like
they are having fun.

"Those nuts look yummy!" says Lolo.

Finish the patterns with a brown crayon.

Look at all the flowers! Lolo finds some butterflies, too.

Color the objects below.

Example

44

Then they see an elephant family.

"This elephant is really big!" says Coz.

Color the animals below.

46

Example

47

Nearby, some hippos take a bath in a pond.

"It's bath time!" says Lolo.

Color the animals below.

Example

Look! A lion family!

Rudi likes the little lion cubs.

Color the animals below.

Example

51

"Gee, I was a little scared," says Coz.
"Let's rest under these nice trees here,"
says Lolo.

Color the trees below.

Example

52

Example

53

"Let's go to the seashore!" says Lolo. Coz starts the car.

Color the car below.

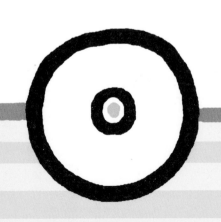

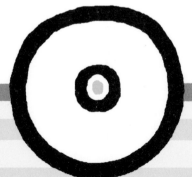

Let's go to the seashore!

The sailboats are colorful.

Color the sails below.

Example

They meet the captain of a big ship. "We are going to leave soon. Please help us make our ship ready!" asks the captain.

Color the ship below.

Example

Look at all the umbrellas on the beach!

Color the umbrellas below.

Example

Example

"Let's go swimming!" says Coz. Color the swimwear below.

Example

Example

"My swimsuit is cute!"
says Lolo.

61

There are so many different shells on the beach!

"I like to collect shells," says Eli.

Color the shells below.

Rudi spots some starfish behind a rock.

"This starfish is really big!" says Coz.

! Color the starfish below.

Example

65

Now the group is floating in the sea. What color should their floats be?

Color the floats below.

Down in the water, there are many jellyfish.

Don't get stung, Rudi!

Color the jellyfish below.

These fish are so pretty!

"What nice colors you have," says Lolo.

Color the fish below.

Example

71

A big wave comes to the beach.

It's a group of whales. Look at them blow water!

Example

Draw the water that the whales are blowing.

Example

73

The ships float by in the sea.
Watch out for the big ship!

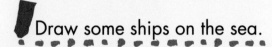 Draw some ships on the sea.

Example

74

Example

The ocean is full of all sorts of life!

What sorts of fish do you see?

Draw some fish in the sea.

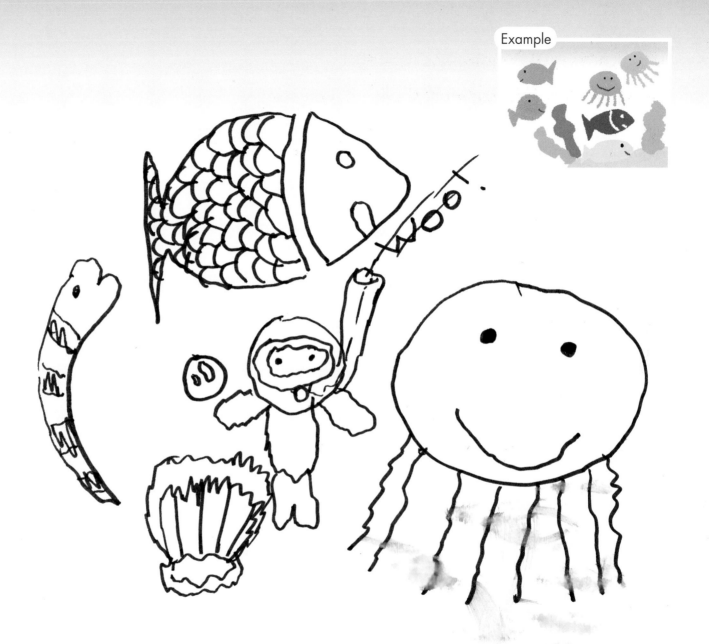

The beach also has many creatures!

What sorts of animals and shells do you see?

Draw some animals and shells on the beach.

Example

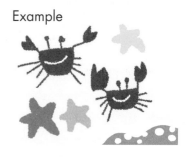

Coz and Lolo had a great time with their many friends.

"Look at all the things we found today!" says Coz.

Draw some things to take home.

Example